Paperback edition first published by Andersen Press in 2020.
First published in Great Britain in 2019 by Andersen Press Ltd.,
20 Vauxhall Bridge Road, London SW1V 2SA.
Copyright © David McKee, 2019.
The right of David McKee to be identified as the author and
illustrator of this work has been asserted by him in accordance
with the Copyright, Designs and Patents Act, 1988.
All rights reserved.
Colour separated in Switzerland by Photolitho AG, Zürich.
Printed and bound in Malaysia.
1   3   5   7   9   10   8   6   4   2
British Library Cataloguing in Publication Data available.
ISBN 978 1 78344 890 6

ELMER'S BIRTHDAY

David McKee

Andersen Press

Elmer, the patchwork elephant, was walking a
morning walk. He said, "Good morning," to a group
of elephants and kept walking.

Once he'd gone, an elephant said, "Tomorrow is
Elmer's birthday. For a joke let's act as if we've
forgotten it. Nobody wish him 'Happy Birthday'.
At the end of the afternoon we'll bring out a cake and
celebrate. We'll have to warn his family and friends or
it won't work."

"I'm not sure it's a good trick," said Bird.
"But if there's cake I'll tell the birds."
The elephants chuckled and hurried off in
different directions to see that nobody said
"Happy Birthday".

When Lion was told, he said,
"Funny kind of joke."
Tiger said, "For Elmer's birthday? But…"
"Please, no buts," said the elephants. "Just
do it," and they hurried off, afraid that
Elmer might appear.

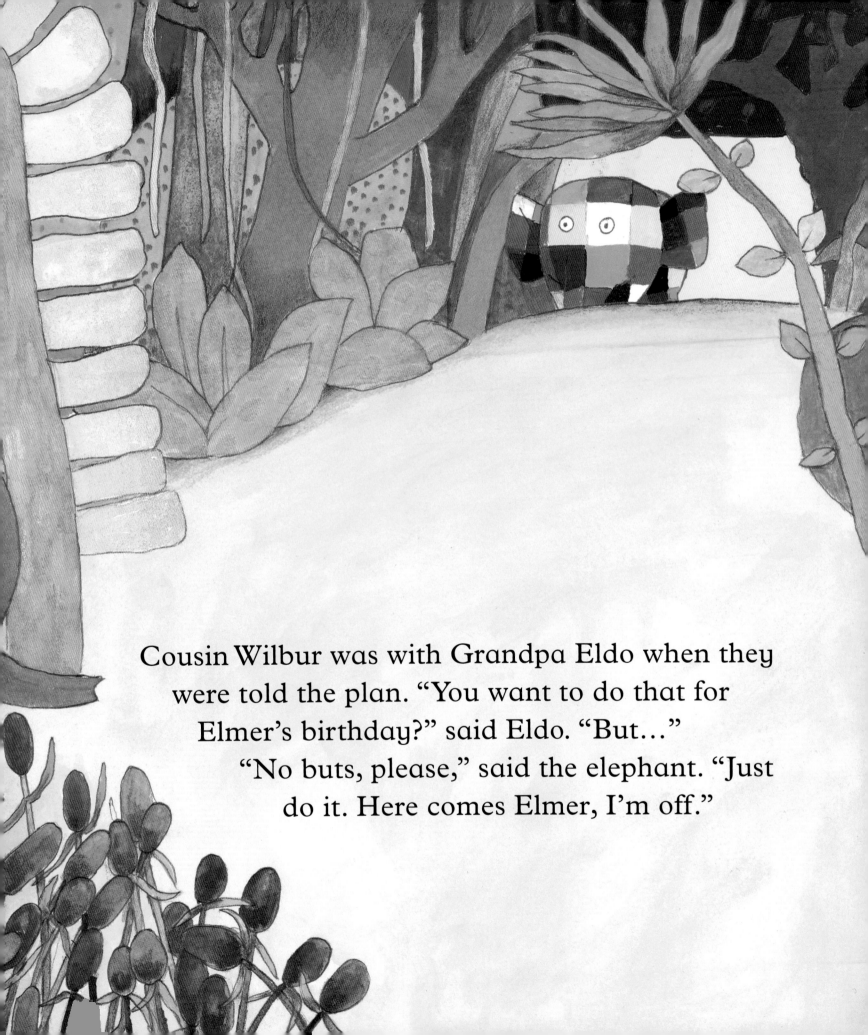

Cousin Wilbur was with Grandpa Eldo when they were told the plan. "You want to do that for Elmer's birthday?" said Eldo. "But…"

"No buts, please," said the elephant. "Just do it. Here comes Elmer, I'm off."

Elmer was nearby when the hippos and crocodiles were told.

"A trick and a cake," said Crocodile. "Whoopee! But…"

"Shush!" said the elephant in a whisper. "Or Elmer will hear. And no buts, just do it."

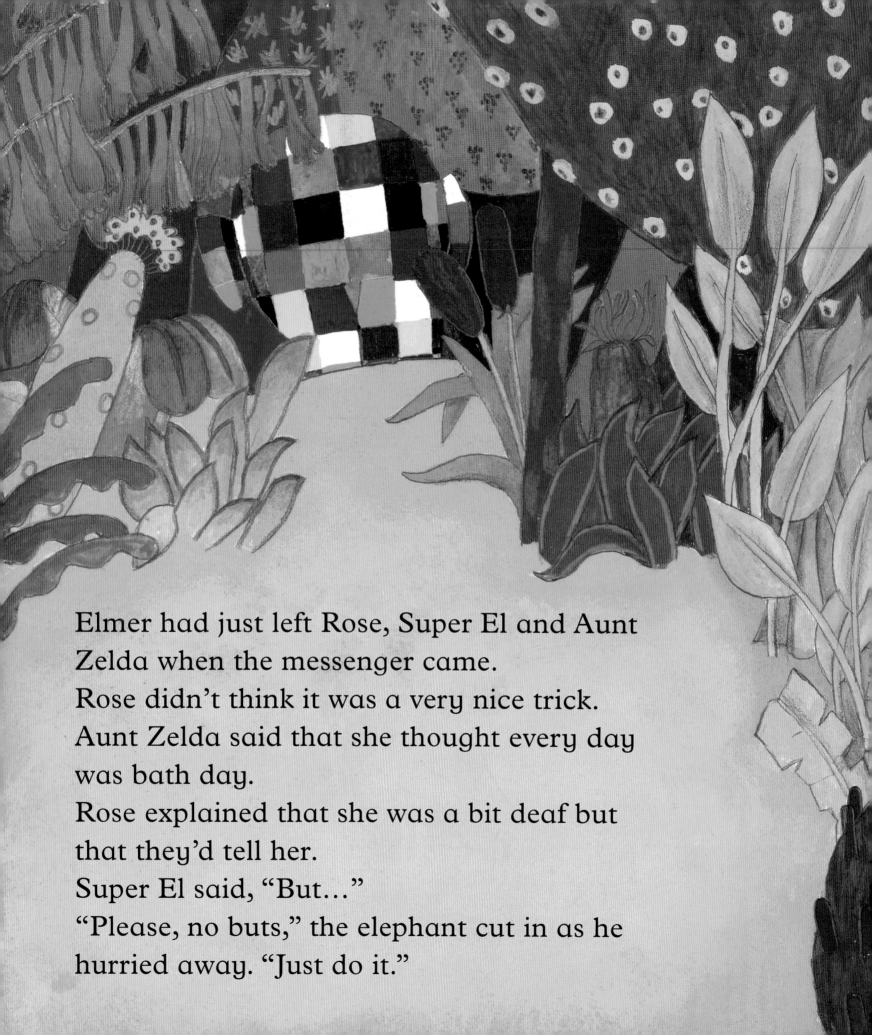

Elmer had just left Rose, Super El and Aunt
Zelda when the messenger came.

Rose didn't think it was a very nice trick.

Aunt Zelda said that she thought every day
was bath day.

Rose explained that she was a bit deaf but
that they'd tell her.

Super El said, "But…"

"Please, no buts," the elephant cut in as he
hurried away. "Just do it."

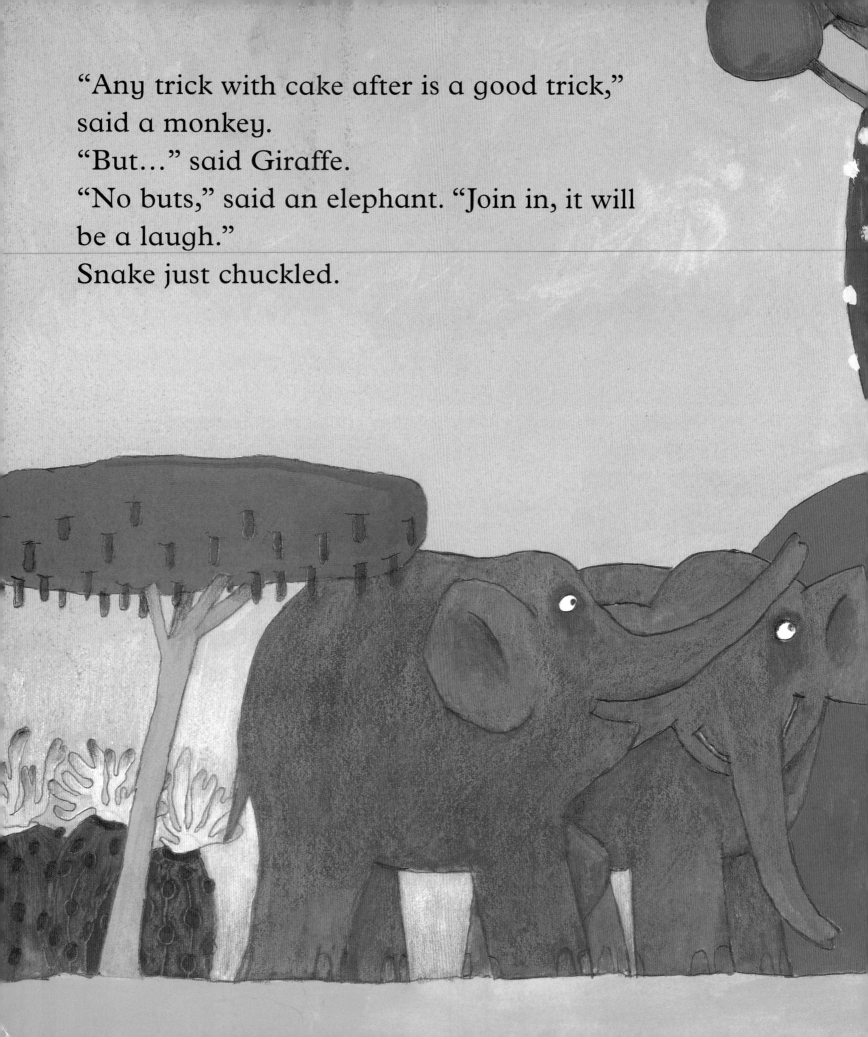

"Any trick with cake after is a good trick," said a monkey.

"But…" said Giraffe.

"No buts," said an elephant. "Join in, it will be a laugh."

Snake just chuckled.

The next day, Elmer went for his usual walk.
He passed some elephants who said, "Good morning,
Elmer," and then sniggered.
He met Lion and Tiger, who said, "Good
morning, Elmer," and didn't snigger but did seem
embarrassed.
"Hmmm!" said Elmer.

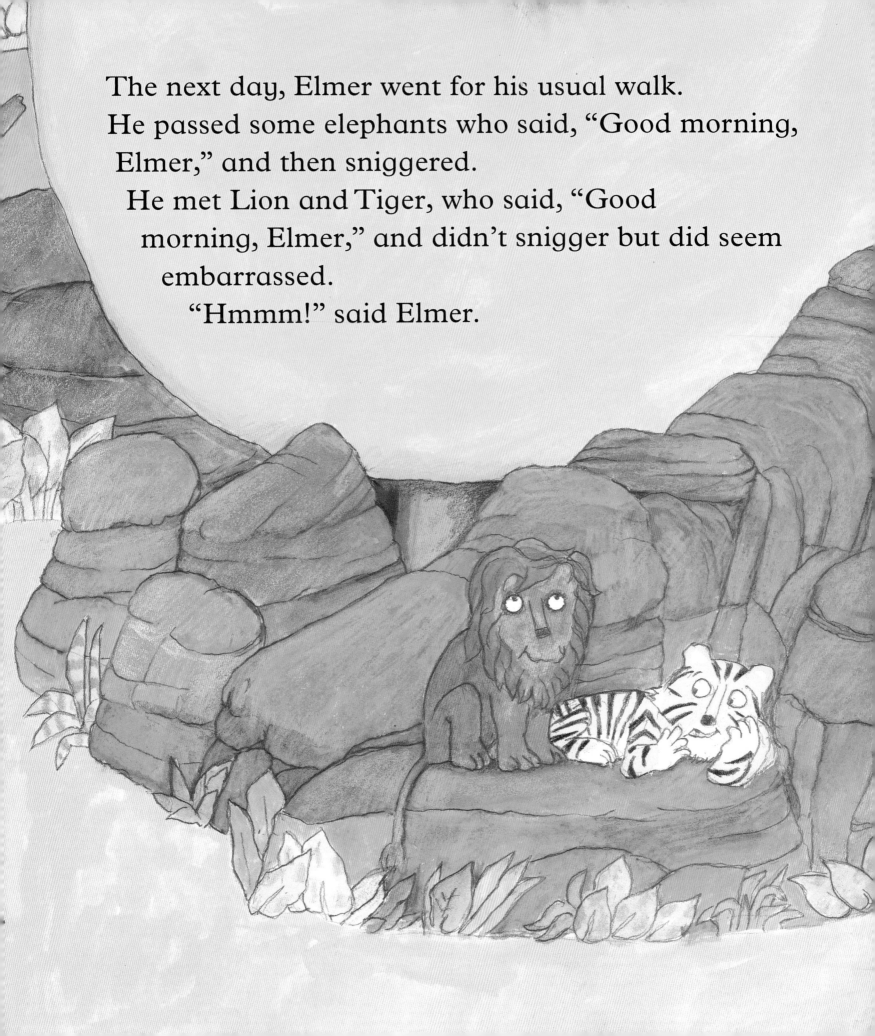

He stopped and chatted with Wilbur who was just
like always.
Some birds flew by and called out, "Good morning, Wilbur.
Good MORNING, Elmer," and flew away giggling.
"Strange," said Elmer.
"Very," said Wilbur.

All day similar things happened. Animals changed direction to avoid Elmer, or hurried past with a quiet "Hello".

At the end of the afternoon, Elmer suddenly found his way blocked by family and friends.

An elephant said, "Elmer, aren't you upset? Nobody has said 'Happy Birthday'."

"But…" said Elmer, "It's not my birthday."

"We tried to tell them," said Tiger, Eldo, Crocodile, Super El and Giraffe. "But they wanted to play a joke."

"And they promised cake," said the monkeys.

"Cake?" said an elephant. "Cake? Whoever heard of elephants baking a cake? That's a real joke."
With that, the elephants brought out a huge cake.

There was silence and then they all burst out laughing.
"Not bad, elephants," said Elmer. "It wasn't a brilliant trick.
It isn't my birthday. But... the cake is a winner."

Read more ELMER stories!

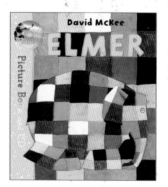

Discover all of ELMER's adventures at:
www.elmer.co.uk